Mem Fox

A Bedtime Story

illustrated by Elivia Savadier

For Salad
—M. F.

To knowing books, loving them,
and sharing them
—E. S.

This edition first published in the United States of America in 1996 by Mondo Publishing
Published in arrangement with MULTIMEDIA INTERNATIONAL (UK) LTD.
Text copyright © 1986, 1996 by Mem Fox
Illustrations copyright © 1996 by Elivia Savadier

For information contact:
MONDO Publishing
One Plaza Road
Greenvale, New York 11548

Printed in Hong Kong by South China Printing Co., (1988) Ltd.
First Mondo printing, February 1996
96 97 97 99 00 01   9 8 7 6 5 4 3 2 1

Designed by Edward Miller
Production by Our House

Library of Congress Cataloging-in-Publication Data
Fox, Mem. A bedtime story/by Mem Fox; illustrated by Elivia Savadier.
Summary: Polly and her friend Bed Rabbit have lots of books, but they don't know how to
read, so Polly's parents interrupt their own reading for a bedtime story.
ISBN 1-57255-136-4. ISBN 1-57255-135-6 (pbk.) [1. Bedtime—Fiction. 2. Books and reading—
Fiction. 3. Toys—fiction. 4. Rabbits—fiction.] I. Savadier, Elivia, ill. II. Title. PZ7.F8373Be 1996
95-33601
[E]—dc20

Once upon a time there was a little girl named Polly who had a friend called Bed Rabbit.

Polly and Bed Rabbit had books here, books there, books and stories everywhere.

Bed Rabbit couldn't read, so one night when Polly wanted to hear a story she called out, "Mom! Dad! Will someone read Bed Rabbit a story, please?"

But Mom and Dad were busy reading their own books. "Have you had your glass of milk?" Dad asked. And quietly carried on reading.

"Yes, I've had my glass of milk," replied Polly, "and so has Bed Rabbit."

"Have you brushed your teeth?" Mom asked. And quietly carried on reading.

"Yes, I've brushed my teeth," replied Polly, "and so has Bed Rabbit."

"Have you been to the bathroom?" Mom asked.
And quietly carried on reading.

"Yes, I've been to the bathroom," replied Polly, "and so has Bed Rabbit."

"Have you got your pajamas on?" Dad asked. And quietly carried on reading.

"Yes, I've got my pajamas on," replied Polly, "and so has Bed Rabbit."

"Are you all snuggled in and ready?" Dad called out.
And quietly carried on reading.

"Yes, I'm all snuggled in and ready," replied Polly, "and so is Bed Rabbit. Isn't anyone coming?"

"Yes, we're coming," said Mom and Dad as they went to Polly's room. There were books here, books there, books and stories everywhere.

Mom and Dad sat down on the bed with Polly and
Bed Rabbit. "This is the one Bed Rabbit wants," said
Polly, and she handed them the story with the scary
pictures. "Once upon a time. . ." began Mom.

And she read and she read until they all lived happily ever after.

"Please read it again," begged Polly. "It makes Bed Rabbit feel scared inside." So Mom read it again.

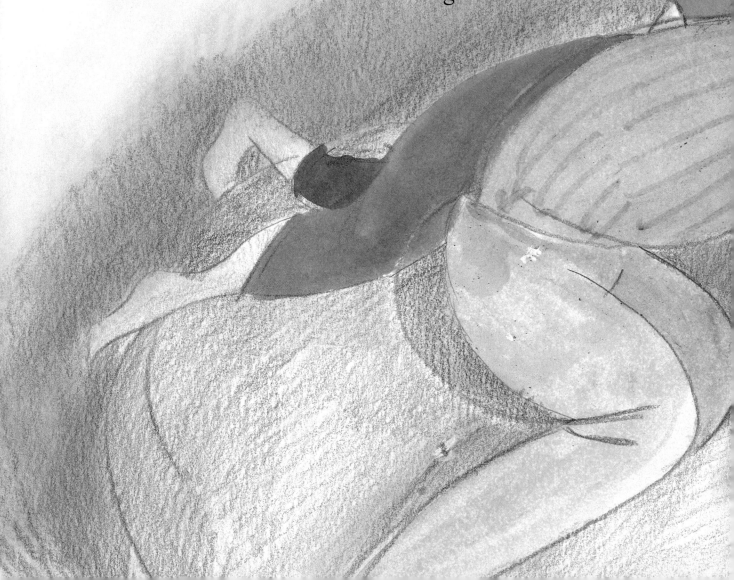

When she closed the book, Polly and Bed Rabbit
were fast asleep. Mom and Dad kissed them both.

"Goodnight, Polly. Goodnight, Bed Rabbit." And Mom and Dad tiptoed together out of the room, and back to their own reading.